Saba & Khushal

Copyright © 2019 by Abu B. Rafique

ISBN: 978-0-359-51123-5

For Fajar.

I.

Khushal watched closely as the smoke he blew out spread across his view of the stars. The thinnest possible veil stretching out over the sky until it wasn't visible anymore, swallowed up entirely by the moonlight. He cleared his throat and took another drag of his cigarette, the glowing ember lighting his tired face for a split second. As they often did on nights when he couldn't sleep, Khushal's thoughts wandered towards his mother. It had been over three years since they'd seen each other or spoken. Save for a letter he had sent to her a year after leaving home, which had been sent back to him without a response.

He wondered what she might be doing at that very moment, if she was asleep, what dreams was she having if she was? And if she wasn't, why was she awake? He finished smoking his cigarette and threw it onto the ground, putting it out with the heel of his sandal before turning around and walking back inside.

Home had existed here before Khushal and Saba had found it. The moment they had stepped inside, both had felt that the little cottage was entirely familiar to them. A place that they might have frequented before, in a time that they could not fully remember. Or perhaps something had pulled them to it all their lives, and never had the feeling been more overwhelming than it had been when they'd first set foot inside.

Even in the dark, Khushal could see every corner of the room clearly, and he deftly moved towards the bedroom. It was just on the opposite end of the glass doors that opened onto the terrace, all the way in the back of the house. When he stepped inside, the floor creaked under him and Saba stirred under the covers. A bit of moonlight slipped its fingers in through a crack in the bedroom curtains, Khushal could see a few locks of hair glowing on her bare shoulder while she slept.

He pulled up the covers to get back in bed beside her, and the momentary exposure caused goosebumps to pop up on the skin of her back and shoulders. Khushal pulled the blankets around them both and then reached out to wrap an arm around her, pulling her towards him gently. Instinctively, Saba turned into him, groaning quietly. "Can't sleep?" she asked without opening her eyes. Khushal didn't answer, instead he leaned down to place a kiss on the top of her head, and put his hand on her shoulder, rubbing it up and down, warming her up again. She returned to her dream within seconds.

Khushal took in the details of her sleeping face. The slightly parted mouth, the eyes that flickered every few seconds, the long lashes brushing her under eyes every time. She had sacrificed as much as he had for what they shared. He knew this. The fact was not lost on him. Yet for some reason, he could not bring himself to talk to her about it. It wasn't that he thought she wouldn't understand, he simply feared that she did not feel the same way about it all. Or, that she might mistake how he felt for regret, which couldn't be further from the truth.

The relationship he had with Saba was something that Khushal had unconsciously moved towards all his life. He knew this deep within the marrow of his marrow, he knew it on the deepest level that a person could possibly know anything.

When he had taken her home to tell his parents that he wanted to marry her, it wasn't his way of asking for permission. It was to declare something he had already made up his mind about. He had expected resistance, but not even he had imagined a reaction as bad as the one they'd gotten. Aziz, his father, had jumped to his feet in an instant and yelled, with every ounce of rage he could muster, "YOU ARE NOT MARRYING THIS GIRL!" and then he had rounded on Laila, his wife, "You see what happens? This whole time you've coddled the boy, and he's been running around like a fool falling in love! This is what he brings home to us!" Laila remained silent, her eyes downcast. Aziz had looked back at Khushal, who was pale, and clutching Saba's hand tightly. The girl herself was glaring at Aziz.

"You don't have my permission," he barked, "Or hers'," he gestured at Laila.

Khushal had cleared his throat, steadying his own voice, "I am not asking you for permission. I am here to tell you that I am going to marry Saba. If you choose to not be there for that, then that is your decision. I will marry her anyway."

"You can get yourself out of this house then, boy! You're no son of mine. Saala bada aashiq aya," Aziz sneered.

Khushal had hesitated. Considering for a moment a rebuttal, something to say. Anything to throw back at the man who, at the moment, he hated more than he had hated anyone else before. But the moment passed. And instead, Khushal shrugged and said, "Fine. Let's go, Saba." And then had turned around and walked out. Pausing on the front step at the sound of glass shattering on the other side of the door. Aziz had flung a plate at the door as they had closed it behind them.

Once they were back in the car, Khushal let out a whimper, and Saba clutched his hands. "It'll be okay," she had whispered, "They'll come around." Khushal shook his head, "He won't. It's not in him." She didn't argue with him, instead Saba squeezed his hands tight and waited while his shaking subsided. "Let's go to yours now," he said finally before starting the car and pulling away from the home.

The reaction at Saba's house had been a little better, until her father asked whether the boy's parents had approved of the union. Very slowly, Khushal had shaken his head. Saba's father, Zakaria, had taken great offense to this. "Does your family think they're too good for us?!" he had asked Khushal, demanding an answer for the ridiculous question. "I don't know. I don't care what they think. I love Saba, I want to marry h-", "YOU don't care?!" Zakaria had roared, cutting the young man off, "You don't care? And who are you? Why should I hand my daughter off to someone who comes from a family that won't even accept her? Absolutely not!"

"Abba, I want to marry him too!" Saba had responded angrily.

"Toh?! This is not how things are done! You stay here from now on, I will find you a boy who deserves you. This worm who can't even convince his own parents is nothing for you!" Zakaria had spit at Khushal's feet following these last words and Khushal had stared at the clump of light brown mucus and saliva that landed near his boots. He loosened his grip on Saba's hand, turned around, and walked out.

Saba had been seething, but she went to her room without much incident, knowing that Khushal would return. And he did.

That night, after everyone else went to bed, she looked through the curtains in her room and saw the glowing ember of a cigarette in the darkness, just a few yards away from the front wall of their home. She opened the window, pushing the door open just enough for the moonlight to be refracted off of it. Ten minutes later, Khushal was perched on the railing of the terrace, right outside her bedroom window.

"So, what now?"

"Well, we had planned for this, hadn't we?"

Khushal nodded, "We did. But what I mean is, do you still want to go through with that?"

"I think I do,"

"You think?"

"I do if you do."

There was a pause before Khushal spoke again, "We're going to be leaving a lot behind."

"They'll come around, Khushal."

"And if they don't?"

This time it was her that hesitated. "Well... we will manage. But I won't let anyone's disapproval keep me from what I want."

"I'm hoping you're referring to me," said Khushal and she smiled before smacking his forehead playfully.

"Still got your bag?" he asked with a grin.

"Mhm."

"Bring it with you then, I'll go start the car."

Khushal had put his own bags in the car that morning before leaving home to pick Saba up from a friend's house. They had spent months planning for this, although they had hoped secretly, and aloud to each other that they wouldn't have to resort to what they had in mind.

In the small mountain town of Afsaan, Saba had visited her grandparents every summer as a girl. It was nestled in a valley, just a few dozen kilometers removed from the region of Kashmir. She had spoken to Khushal about it many times on many sleepless nights, talking about how she dreamed of having a home there herself one day. The grandparents were gone, but the dream remained. And so that was where they went.

A day of driving and they finally stopped in front of a house belonging to an old childhood friend of Saba's. A friend who had agreed to house them until they could become situated, a friend who had agreed to be a witness. Khushal went into town and paid a cleric to conduct the ceremony. A few more people were gathered to be witnesses. Saba and Khushal bathed and dressed in the nicest clothes they had brought with them. He dressed in a pressed navy-blue suit, his dark hair and thin mustache both combed through and still smelling faintly of the rose soap he had used to bathe with. And her, dressed in a gold dress adorned with dozens of silver ornaments, the veil on her head held in place by the red and gold tika resting on her forehead, and her eyes darkened with kohl. Twenty-four hours after arriving, the two were married.

It took them only three weeks to find their new home. Saba's friend had told them that on the other side of town there was an old cottage that been built during the time of the British. It had fallen into disrepair in the decades since and served more as a relic in the town now than anything else. Occasionally, travelers passing through would find shelter there for a night or two. But other than that, it wasn't used anymore. The land itself and its upkeep were the responsibility of the owner of the local library. His family had thrived when the British presence had been there, but their power and influence waned after Independence. He himself chose to pursue his own goals in life, leaving his parents without an heir. They had willed the land to him before their deaths, and he kept it only to respect their dying wish.

Khushal had approached the man with an offer, and the bored old man had simply countered with, "If you can fix the old place up, it's yours."

With the help of a few locals, the cottage was restored to a semblance of its former splendor by the end of the summer. They painted the walls a calm shade of blue, in the bright light of the sun or the moon, the house almost looked like it was glowing. The polished wooden floors still held the drag marks of large pieces of furniture that had been moved across it over the years. The walls were painted with a pattern of every single flower native to the valley attached to thin black vines curling out and upwards from every corner of every room. The sunlight streaming in through the open windows and doors caught the particles of dust floating around, making the air shimmer. The familiarity they both felt was contained in this dust. She pushed him up against an old bookshelf in the corner of the sitting room and kissed him. "It's a dream," she had said breathlessly, "Just like a dream." Khushal smiled and reached down to lift her up, carrying her to their new bedroom.

The two had found work at the local school as teachers. Saba had taught in the city, she was the experienced one and took to her new job the way a bird took to flight. Khushal was the one who struggled, but he was learning. He would watch her while she taught, taking in how she interacted with her students, how she spoke to them, explained to them.

In the evenings they would make love by the fireplace. The house dark, save for the glow that wrapped itself around them. She would lay there in his arms afterwards, aware of the fact that a thousand thoughts were turning over each other in his mind. She felt the same way but didn't know how to say it.

"I love you," she would say in an attempt to put it all into the three words.

"I love you too," he would respond, failing at the task himself.

And as he watched her sleep, Khushal felt he could see fragments of the dreams that she was having. He wanted to wake her up. To ask her about them. To talk about what he'd been thinking about. But he couldn't, not yet anyway.

It would have to wait.

The morning was just a few hours away.

They would have tea together then.

It could wait.

He leaned down and kissed her mouth softly. Then he lowered his head to the pillow and drifted off to sleep.

Laila awoke with a start.

Her hand moved instinctively to the talisman she wore around her neck. The stitching that held the leather square together was soft and worn under her fingers. She had been dreaming of Khushal. Most nights, he was all that she dreamt of. "Dreams" were an inaccurate summation of what she saw when asleep. There were flashes of his childhood that she remembered, blurred, distorted, making her unsure of *when* she was, rather than where. There were other, clearer memories of his adolescence. Learning how to drive, his first job, his graduation. And then there were things that she didn't recognize, but she didn't feel that they were dreams either. Glimpses of hills and mountainous terrain, an axe hitting wood, a small classroom. And then the girl.

Saba was her name.

For whatever reason, Laila sometimes saw her as clear as day in situations that she had no reason to imagine the girl in.

She didn't know what it all meant, or even what exactly it all was. But she did know that she missed Khushal terribly. And that lone fact was the reason for what she saw.

Laila turned to her side to see her husband's back facing her. His nightshirt was taut across his back as he slept, his deep snores filled the air. Her waking had not bothered his sleep in the slightest, which didn't surprise her. Whatever bond exists within a marriage, be it love or otherwise, had broken long ago between the two of them. But they were both too old to remove themselves from the labels attached to them. Husband and Wife. Aziz played his role, Laila played hers'.

The final straw had been the last time they had seen Khushal. Aziz had kicked him out without second thought when he had brought the girl home to them, to tell them he planned on marrying her. A day later they received a phone call from the girl's father, he was yelling that his daughter was missing.

It didn't take a long while with the police to determine that Khushal and Saba had run away together.

"Would you like to file a kidnapping charge?" the inspector had asked Saba's father. "She WANTED to marry him!" Aziz had countered before the other man, Zakaria, could answer. "I don't think my daughter would run off with a boy unless she was made to," said Zakaria. "SHE STOOD RIGHT HERE AND CAME TO US WANTING TO MARRY HIM!" Aziz roared. Another policeman held him back as he moved towards Zakaria. "So you say, but your son is nowhere to be found. And my daughter was in her room alone, last time I checked. That boy of yours came back in the middle of the night and took her through her window," Zakaria refused to back down.

In the end, a kidnapping charge had been filed, with orders to arrest Khushal if anyone saw him in the city again. A few posters were printed and plastered all over the city, over the hundreds of others. The officers really did not care much for what they knew was probably a case of the young couple running off together to marry. Something they saw countless times. If a girl's family was rich enough, they might track the boy down and arrest him, rough him up for a few days until the girl's family could marry her off to someone else, and then let him go. But most of the time, cases like these were handed off to younger, newer deputies. Something to make them feel like they were doing something while they still held onto their idealizations of "making a difference."

Laila stared at Aziz's back, knowing somehow that it was unlikely that Khushal would ever be coming back. No arrest would be made. Her son would be fine. But he was away from her still, and that was something she could not understand how to cope with. All her life, she had lived with some sense of devotion to someone. First, it was her parents and her family. She was devoted to the role of a good daughter, and when it was decided that she should be married, she agreed to it without much fuss. She was old enough, she had finished her schooling. And she wasn't being forced into anything with anyone. All she had to do was say that she didn't like the boy, and her parents would politely decline the proposal.

Aziz had seemed nice when she had first met him. Polite, a little shy, and oddly charming. He was tall too, and handsome in those days. It was before the poison of his ill temperament had permanently soured his face. In those days he was bright, maybe even happy. Although she couldn't remember now if such a description truly fit the Aziz she had married, or if she had just dreamt it up over the years to bring some sense of peace to her own recollections.

After her marriage, she had been devoted to him. Being the good wife, keeping him happy, supporting him when he needed it, cooking what he liked, maintaining her appearance, all for him. It was strangely a lonely existence, even though it depended entirely on the presence of another. Aziz hadn't mistreated her in any way in those first few years, but he simply might not have been there at all, it wouldn't have made a difference.

Perhaps he hadn't ever learned how to show any love that he felt, perhaps he didn't even love her. Whatever the reason, the marriage seemed like nothing, nothing but a bond filled with loneliness.

There had been one instance, one she knew she hadn't imagined or dreamed. They had gone on a walk after dinner one evening, and after stepping back in through their front gate and shutting it behind them, Aziz had suddenly put a hand on her shoulder. When Laila turned to look at him, he leaned in and kissed her on the mouth. It was quick contact. No passion in it, no desire. It was a practiced kiss. And then he gave her another, this time grabbing her waist clumsily with his hands. She stared at his face wide eyed during the act, there wasn't time for her to kiss back, she kept her lips pressed together instead.

Once he pulled away, Laila blinked and smiled at him kindly. Aziz cleared his throat and looked down.

"Where did that come from?" she asked him.

"I, um, I enjoyed the walk we had," he mumbled without looking up at her.

"It was nice, yes."

"I like having you for my wife, Laila."

She hesitated, the lie was ready to leap from her tongue, but still she hesitated. Just for a moment before saying, "I like having you for my husband."

Part of her had hoped that the poorly executed act of affection was the start of some change. Maybe it had just taken a while. Maybe she had judged too quickly.

But no.

Aziz had embarrassed himself. And he did not know how to deal with that. He had wanted to show his wife something more than what he knew. These gestures of love, tenderness, the stuff of flowery poetry written by wine drunk men and women filled with sadness, none of these were things he understood. And his one attempt had failed.

Laila would've understood, had any of this been said out loud. But it wasn't. Aziz fell into himself. And Laila put a wall between them both.

They spoke.

They ate.

They lived together.

They shared a bed.

Occasionally they made loveless love.

And that was it.

That was life.

As she remembered the old days, Laila felt a chill go through her body. The minimal amount of sweat that had collected on the body during sleep had cooled since she had pulled her blankets away. And now she was cold.

Very quietly, she slipped out of bed, and eased her way out of the bedroom. Once the door had been pulled shut behind her, she turned around and flicked on the light at the bottom of the stairs. Her eyes adjusted to the glow as she descended. She blinked twice at the foot of the stairs to clear the bursts of color erupting in front of her eyes, and then turned into the kitchen.

Laila quietly brewed herself a cup of tea, she sat at the little table in the corner of the kitchen, sipping it slowly while eyeing the clock on the wall. It wasn't even three am yet. She closed her eyes and placed her chin on her hands.

The third, and strongest, sense of devotion that Laila felt in her life was to Khushal. The moment she had laid eyes on her son just before losing consciousness in the hospital, her heart had bound itself to him. The miserable existence with Aziz didn't matter, the boy filled the empty spaces where joy should have been. Every new breath of life, every new day that Khushal gained, it all filled her heart as a payment for what she endured.

As he grew older she felt she had a deeper bond with him than what was deemed normal. She could tell when the boy was hurt or upset, even if he wasn't near her. She could feel when he was nearby even without him making his presence known. Her mother told her that such a thing was normal for a parent, especially a mother, and that she herself shared something similar with Laila and her other children, but Laila knew this was something more. Her dreams and her senses too prophetic to simply be another maternal bond.

But in the years since he'd left, she felt that her connection to him had waned. She had no control anymore, no clear understanding of what she felt or saw in her dreams. It was a blur, a manifestation of just how much she missed him. Something had broken between them when he left home, not *because* he left, but why and how he did it. She wondered often if Khushal felt this way too, but she had no way of knowing. He had sent her a letter years before, Aziz had seen it and sent it back without giving her a chance to answer.

Of course, when looking at her own life and her marriage, Laila could not be happier that her son had fallen in love with someone he wanted to be with. Someone who, more importantly, wanted to be with him as well. Perhaps it was easier for men. They had more time to pick and choose, and they were encouraged to do just that. Regardless, Laila could not hate him for his decision. Nor could she hate the girl he'd fallen for.

The name Saba was still foreign on her tongue, even though the girl had most likely been her daughter-in-law for years now. She did not know the girl enough. The name was almost that of a stranger. And sometimes Laila felt that the reason why her bond with Khushal had deteriorated so much was because he too was now a stranger. She did not know Khushal the Man in Love. Khushal the Husband. She only knew her son. Someone might have forgotten to tell her all those years ago, but children do not remain that forever. They are never bound to what their parents see when they look at them, they are never bound to their parents. For twenty-two years he had filled the gaps, but now he was gone. And those empty spaces were larger than ever. They were filled with enough loneliness for Laila to drown herself in.

And she was almost certain that if such a thing were to happen, nobody would notice at all.

Khushal's lower back burned as he planted his feet and swung his axe downward. There was a heavy "thunk" sound as it made contact with the wood, splitting it neatly into two pieces. He had not slept very long, just a few hours. He'd woken up as the earliest light of dawn was beginning to peek out over the horizon in the distance. After trying for a few minutes to go back to sleep, Khushal had finally given up, gotten out of bed, retrieved his axe from the shed, and busied himself at the tree line a few yards down from the cottage.

The moon was full and still hanging high in the pink, early morning sky, but just for a little while longer. Soon it would dip below the horizon, the sun having risen fully. Khushal stood there for a moment, catching his breath, staring at the moon. He was acutely aware of the steam that rose up from his exposed arms in the warm glow of the rising sun.

"How many hours was that? More or less than usual?" Saba's voice cut into his trance. Khushal turned to see her standing there with a maroon shawl wrapped tightly around her shoulders and a light-yellow scarf resting loosely on her head. He set the axe down and wiped his sweaty, dirt stained hands on the legs of his pajamas. "It was probably less," he said as he walked over and wrapped his arms around her. Saba clicked her tongue and put both hands on his chest, staring at his face. "I'm worried about you, janan. You sleep even less than usual all the time now. Why won't you tell me what it is that's keeping you up?" Khushal shook his head and sighed heavily, "I'm not sure what it is myself. It's just a feeling. This feeling in the back of my mind. It makes me worry, but I can't figure out what it is." The look on Saba's face was one of deep concern. Khushal kissed her cheek, "I promise if I knew what it was, I would tell you. I *will* tell you if I figure it out. I can't hide anything from you, joonam."

Saba looked at him, taking in the beads of sweat on his face, the way his mouth moved as he formed his words. She believed him. She knew he wasn't lying to her, that was something he never did. They never kept things from each other, but she knew that sometimes Khushal took a little longer to come around and say what he felt. And for this, she had no solution. She had nothing she could say or do to ease his mind. "Did you find any lies in all that scanning?" Khushal asked her casually as she went through these thoughts, Saba smiled and put her head on his chest, "No." And then she leaned up and kissed his cheek, "Come in and have breakfast with me, I have to be at the school a little earlier today," she said. "I'll be right in," said Khushal, "let me finish here." "Janan, there's enough wood to last us and the whole town three winters, at least. Come inside," she tugged on the crook of his elbow and he took a step forward reluctantly. "Alright," he said as he leaned in to kiss her.

As they began walking back towards the house they saw that Hamza Mian, the old man who lived on the other side of the hill, was shuffling in their direction. He had a skullcap pulled taut over his shaved head. He had just finished his Fajr prayers at the mosque. Every morning after the prayers, the old man would walk from the mosque, past his own home, past Saba and Khushal's home, and down the hill into town where he owned and operated his own shop of homeopathic medicines. His frail arm went up in a wave at the young couple as he approached. "Salaam!" he called out. "Walaikum Asalam!" said Saba and Khushal together. Hamza Mian stopped once he was a few feet away and coughed into a maroon handkerchief he kept folded up in the breast pocket of his muslin shirt.

"You should be wearing more layers, Uncle. The weather is getting colder and colder," said Saba.

Hamza Mian waved a hand at her, "No need to worry about that yet, beti. I've been through more winters here than you'll experience in your lifetime," he smiled, "You city kids still need to adjust a bit more. This cough of mine is something that comes and goes with age. I am blessed. I could be much worse. Aging is a nasty thing, you'll come to see." Hamza Mian paused to cough again before clearing his throat and looking at Khushal, "I did not see you at the mosque for prayers this morning, beta." Khushal's sweaty face flushed even more and he muttered the words, "I was chopping wood."

"Of course, it is the pious who rise early to work and take advantage of the day He has given us. Magar, you mustn't forget, remembering Him when we're supposed to is just as important," said the old man sagely.

Khushal nodded and Saba fought back the urge to smile as she watched her husband squirm under the brief lecture. But then Hamza Mian smiled, "Ah, but He must find you to be deserving of blessings anyway. Look at the wife He has given you. Look at the paradise you live in."

"We never forget how fortunate we are, Uncle," said Saba with a big smile, "And we have good people like you to remind us if we ever do," she tugged on Khushal's arm, and they began walking again. "Please come by for tea sometime soon, one day when we aren't working," she said.

Hamza Mian bowed his head slightly at the retreating couple, "Of course, beti. Of course." And then he waved again before resuming his own walk towards his shop.

"The man makes me feel like the biggest sinner alive," said Khushal as they neared the fence to their back garden. "Well, is he wrong?" Saba teased. Khushal smiled, "You pray enough for the both of us. What could I say that you don't already?"

"I don't always pray either, janan."

"Yes. But *he* doesn't know that."

"If women could pray in the mosque, he might."

"Such a radical notion you present, joonam," teased Khushal.

Saba nudged him with her elbow and he laughed, holding the door open for her before following her into the house.

Later that day, Khushal went to the market while Saba was still at the school. He only had to teach one class that day. He read poetry to his students from one of the many second-hand collections he kept in his classroom, and then had the students spend the remainder of the class crafting poems of their own. He enjoyed teaching the younger students. When he covered things like story writing or poetry in the class, they didn't ask many questions the way the older students did. They simply took to the work naturally. Even the least imaginative of the children could create such vivid imagery with the simplest of words. Of course, Saba was able to handle students of every age, at every level. Khushal found it harder to explain certain things to the older students. They wanted to know why. Always the why. And he didn't always have the answer, he couldn't explain things in a way that they could all understand.

In school he himself had studied literature, thrown himself into whatever novel or poem came his way. He had learned best that way. He had whittled his own skills into something worth admiring. But none of this meant that he was a good teacher. He did not have the passion needed for it, the way Saba did. For him, it was simply a way to earn money and a way to continue being with her. She often told him to find other work, at an office in town, or maybe even working with any of the numerous laborers who worked from sunrise until sunset every day. His woodcutting a testament to his physical capability. But he always refused, stating that if worked a job that exhausted him, he'd be too tired to spend time with her in the evenings.

One of the many ways in which Saba and Khushal were alike was in their affinity for the night. They both came alive as the sun set, and when most people were turning into bed, the young couple was finding something to do. Even before they had met each other, this is how they had been.

In the city, they would often meet up late at night after sneaking out and go to see a late-night film. Or maybe dine at one of the many roadside stalls frequented by truckers passing through in the midnight hours for a delicious hot meal. They would make delightful conversation with the truckers over sizzling pots of spiced lamb, chicken, and fresh, soft naan.

Since moving to the valley, their activities might have changed, but their habit remained the same. They would go on late night walks, exploring the town after the bulk of its residents had gone to bed. The ones they ran into who were still awake would often invite the young couple in for cups of tea and some storytelling or gossip. Or they would get in the car and drive to the hills overlooking the woods that led to the mountains on the other side. Sometimes they'd build a fire and spend hours laying there under the stars, or Khushal would pull out his gun and he and Saba would take turns firing into the nighttime horizon.

Other nights they would stay home, Khushal would light a fire in the fireplace and they would lie in front of it together. They would read to each other sometimes, or else they'd reminisce on things they'd done together, or before they had met each other.

For that night, Khushal had decided he would cook Saba's favorite chicken curry for dinner before she got home. They could see where the night took them after that. He pulled his shawl tighter around himself as he walked through the market, pausing to greet the locals he knew and engage in snippets of small-talk as he gathered what he would need. "Khushal Babu is playing the housewife today, huh?" joked Aniqa-Ji, the aging grin missing the two bottom front teeth. Khushal laughed politely and nodded, "I'm not made for teaching the way Saba is, Aniqa-Ji."

"You should have seen the way he was chopping wood this morning," Hamza Mian said to Aniqa-Ji, "He could chop enough wood for the whole valley to burn all winter long and not be tired at all by the end of it!"

"You're telling tales, Uncle," said Khushal.

Hamza Mian shook his head, "It's true. It is rare to see that kind of power in a boy from the city. You were made for to live in a place like this, I think."

"Or maybe this valley was made for me," said Khushal, "Or maybe it was made for Saba and I both."

"This filmy talk! I don't want to hear i! Pah!" Aniqa-Ji shook her head, her cheeks quivering with the movement of her head, "Take this and go!" She shoved the bag of vegetables he had paid for into his hands and shooed him away. "What is wrong with love, Aniqa-Ji?!" Khushal was grinning now. "Love is the game of the young and the foolish!" she shouted back, "Don't bring it here, we are too old for it!"

Khushal was so immersed in his errands that he did not notice the short man wrapped in the dusty blue shroud who was watching him from the opposite street corner near the barbershop. The man was looking at the picture Zakaria had provided him and the other men. There was a thick mustache and a bit of a beard on the boy's face now, but it was him.

It was Khushal.

The man grinned to himself, his slightly yellowed teeth glistening with spit. He dialed a number on his mobile phone and held it up to his ear.

"What is it?" a voice on the other end answered gruffly.

"Asalam walaikum. I have wonderful news. We are about to get paid," there was no hiding the glee in his own voice for the man.

"What are you talking about, Imran? Speak sense or I'll hang up."

"I have found the boy. The one that Zakaria Saab asked us to find."

Immediately, the tone on the other end changed to one of excitement, "Are you sure it's him?! Don't make any mistakes, we can't afford a mistake with this!"

"I'm sure. I'm absolutely certain it's him. He has grown his beard out, but it's him."

"Send us the location then. We'll head out early tomorrow morning."

"I don't see the girl with him."

"It doesn't matter. We need the boy; the girl will follow."

Saba barely noticed the girls waving good-bye to her near the school gate. It wasn't until one of them shouted, "Miss Saba!" that she blinked and turned her head to see them standing there against the red brick columns, coats pulled snugly over their school uniforms. Saba smiled and waved at them through the crowd rushing past. She wondered if she should wait back and make sure the girls were picked up by their parents, but then she quickly pushed the thought of her mind. There were other teachers all around the courtyard, as well as the guards on the other side of the gate. The girls would be fine.

This was something she still wasn't completely used to. In a town so small, everyone knew each other, there was hardly ever a need to keep such a close eye out. Except during the winter season, when the heavy snowfall and blistering, cold winds would make going outdoors a risky task for anyone. It was a slower, more structured way of life, less random and chaotic than the lifestyle that existed back home in the city. Or in any city anywhere, for that matter.

And so, after waving at the girls, Saba pulled her scarf up lightly over her head and buttoned up her coat before walking out of the school's courtyard. One of the guards saw her and bowed his head slightly by way of good-bye and she smiled at him as she walked by. Home was not too far away, only ten- or fifteen-minutes walking. Most days, she and Khushal walked to and from the school together. But today he had left early, she knew, as he sometimes did. Sometimes it was to run errands, other times it was to chop wood, and every once in a while he would simply go home and lay down, sleep coming to him finally at the strangest of hours.

Lately, a divide of sorts had formed between the two of them. Something was in the air, nagging at them both, nesting in the backs of their minds to gnaw away at their thoughts whenever they had a moment to spare. Saba had a feeling it was influencing his dreams, it was affecting hers' as well. Yet for whatever reason, they both seemed unable to talk about it. At first, she had thought that maybe it was because they were getting close to their anniversary, a day that was incredibly happy, but also brought with it the memories of everything they had both left behind. Saba, at least, still spoke to her mother. The woman would call twice a month, all the way from America. And she and Saba would talk until the minutes on the calling card ran out. Khushal did not maintain contact with his family, and she knew this pained him. After some time had passed, however, she knew that it was something more.

It wasn't just their anniversary, there was this sense of dread she had in the pit of her stomach. Something that she hardly noticed except for when she would have moments to herself. It was then that it would crash down onto her like a sudden wave, making her head spin, and an overwhelming feeling of sadness grip every single one of her senses. The inability to communicate this to Khushal made her feel incredibly lonely. She was sure that the block would pass. She had always believed in what she shared with him, never had a doubt entered her mind. And she knew that he felt the same way. Saba was convinced that if multiple lives were a true concept, then she had known him in each one. The bond between them was too strong to shake that belief. And who was to say such a love couldn't exist? Thousands of stories and poems had been written about this kind of love over the centuries, they had to be based on something.

Her thoughts carried her all the way home, she was finally pulled out of them by the warm smell of a fresh cooked meal when she stepped into the cottage. Khushal smiled at her from the stove where he was slowly stirring a pot. "I wanted to cook outside, but it's getting too damn cold out there." "Is my city babu too weak to handle the rough and tumble mountain weather?" Saba teased as she strode over and wrapped her arms around his neck. "Keep up the jokes, see if I let you have any of this," he wrapped an arm around her waist while still stirring with his other hand. Saba glanced into the pot and grinned. "My favorite!" "I figured you needed it," Khushal smiled at her and kissed the top of her head.

"What makes you say that?" Saba broke their embrace and began pulling off her gloves and coat. "Things just feel down lately, I don't know."

She paused and looked up at him, his attention had returned to his cooking. "Hey," she spoke quietly, "Look at me." Khushal looked up and over at her, Saba leaned in over the countertop beside him and he smiled. His eyes were bloodshot, his exhaustion evident in them. "What do you mean by that?" she asked. He sighed and turned down the heat on the stove before crossing his arms and coming around to where she was standing. He took her hands in his own and gently placed his forehead against hers'. "I'm not sure," he said with his eyes closed, "It's just this rotten feeling. It's everywhere. And I know you feel it too."

"I was thinking about it just now, on the way home." "It's what's been keeping me up even more than usual the past few weeks. I feel like something terrible is about to happen," Khushal opened his eyes looked at her, "I don't know if it's about to happen to Amma, or to you, or maybe someone we both know. I don't know. I don't know what it is but it feels like this weight on my chest." She listened to him speak and gently placed a hand on his chest, "Maybe it's just the season, janan." "Do you feel it too?" "I'm not sure what I'm feeling exactly, but it is similar to that, yes. That something bad might happen soon." "So, what do we do?"

For a moment, the sound of the chicken curry bubbling on the stove was the only sound, and then Saba sighed and kissed Khushal on the cheek. "We wait. We wait for the feeling to pass, or for whatever is going to happen to just happen, and then we deal with it together." Khushal smiled and nodded silently, not knowing what else to say.

"I'm going to go change while you finish up here."

"It'll be ready soon."

As she walked to the bathroom, Saba smiled. The feeling was still there somewhere, but the brief conversation about it with Khushal had put her fears at ease for the time being.

II.

Zakaria felt a sense of triumph surging through his whole body as he hung up the phone. It was almost midnight and Iftikhar had called to tell him that they had found the boy, Khushal. His daughter had not been seen, but it was the boy that Zakaria wanted. As he pushed himself out of his seat, a low groan passed through his lips. Very slowly, Zakaria paced around his study. Rasul Khan, his servant, had added some more wood to the fire in the fireplace before turning in for the night, and it still burned brightly in the otherwise darkened room. This study had belonged to Zakaria's grandfather, who had first built the manor back when the British still reigned over the subcontinent. In those days, the family had owned a large amount of the surrounding lands. But over the decades, pieces of it had been bought off for various reasons, or else divided unevenly amongst members of the family. Zakaria had been left with the manor, which lost some of its extravagance when compared to the newer homes, manors, and mansions owned by the elite of the elite in society. But it was still a grand and beautiful home. A relic of the past nestled in comfortably amongst the newer, faster, and ever-growing city. Time had not yet reclaimed it, but ever since his daughter had left, Zakaria felt that it was on the verge of doing just that any day now.

He was not very old, not even sixty. But there was more grey than brown in his hair now, and old injuries resurfaced in the form of constant aches. Zakaria felt the weight of aging, when he had turned fifty years old he had found solace in the fact that once Saba came of age and he found a suitable husband for her, she would inherit the home. As well as his businesses and other plots of land that belonged to him throughout the country. It was unusual, but not unheard of for a daughter to receive so much inheritance, and a man in Zakaria's position could make sure that any disapprovals of his decision would not harm Saba in the slightest.

The two dark days of his life came one after the other.

First, Zakaria's wife, Naiha, left him. Theirs' had been a marriage arranged by Zakaria's father. He had summoned Zakaria to the study one evening nearly thirty years prior. At the time, the young man had just graduated with honors from his university in London, he had returned home for a break before deciding what to do next with his life. His father, Mehmood Bhatt, was a soft spoken but serious man. He rarely needed to raise his voice for anything, his presence was commanding enough. Without changing his tone, the man could give congratulations to a newlywed couple and order a local gangster to beat up the bride to be's former lover in the same sentence.

It was in this same calm tone that he said to Zakaria, "I have found you a wife." Zakaria had expected his parents to find him a wife, but not so soon. "She is well educated. Only a year younger than you, comes from a very good family. I have conducted business with her father's advertising company over the past few months, he and his wife have agreed to the match as well. They're talking to the girl tonight, as I am with you." Zakaria stared at his father, his brain numb, words were trying miserably to make their way to his mouth. "Speak, boy." At the command, Zakaria was finally able to clear his throat and ask, "What's she look like?" His father had smiled at this and come around with a photograph of the girl in his hand.

The two were married that summer, meeting only a few times prior to the wedding itself. The first few months together had passed by blissfully, the two seemed like a perfect match. Naiha was vivacious, intelligent, kind, and incredibly beautiful. Zakaria found himself at ease with her, laughing at her playful teasing, being affectionate in a way he had never imagined for himself. He had been with other women before, but those had been the quick and fumbled meetings of those who were inexperienced and trying their hardest to hold back every ounce of vulnerability that they could. On the wedding night, when Zakaria had held Naiha's face in his hands, she had smiled at their trembling. And when his turban bumped the veil on her head because he'd forgotten to take both off beforehand, they had both burst out laughing.

Then one weekend, when they were staying at the manor instead of in the flat they had a few miles away, Mehmood pulled Zakaria aside while the women were having their post breakfast tea, squeezed his shoulder firmly, and said, "You two are a good match. And this was something I should have told you before the wedding, but she cannot overshadow you. A man must command respect from everyone, including his wife."

And that was that.

Since that day, things slowly changed between the two. Arguments and big fights became common. Usually ending with Naiha screaming that Zakaria was suffocating her before slamming the door to the bedroom and locking it. The only relatively peaceful period that came after that was when she had been pregnant with Saba. A small part of her had been nervous that a daughter would earn nothing but disapproval from Zakaria, but she'd been pleasantly surprised when he'd stepped into the delivery room and beamed at both her and the baby girl in her arms.

Saba was adored by both her parents. No matter how much they fought, or how angry they were with each other, Naiha and Zakaria always set it all aside to dote on their daughter. Naiha established firmly that she did not want to have another child with Zakaria, he was fine with this. As far as he was concerned, his daughter was enough. A month after Saba's tenth birthday, Zakaria started what would become their last fight. Naiha had gotten drunk at a dinner party held at the home for some of Zakaria's clients.

"It's not becoming of a woman to drink like that! People will think my wife is an alcoholic!"

"Let them! If I am an alcoholic it's because I'm married to you! What do you care what I do or don't do unless it affects the perfect little image your Baba created for you?!"

They'd gone back and forth like this for half the night, and finally gone to bed not speaking to each other. The following day, Zakaria regarded her with a silent fury. It all came forth in one big burst during dinner that night when Naiha finally snapped, "How much longer are you going to brood like a petulant child?"

Zakaria had flung his plate at the wall, and Naiha had thrown her glass in response. Both became acutely aware of the fact that Saba was still in the room, eyeing her parents with fear in her eyes. Rasul Khan came running into the room and grabbed the girl, gently pulling her out of the room while taking in the sight of the couple glaring at each other with pure loathing in their eyes. "Let's go betiya, up to your room now. Let your parents speak..."

Once the door closed behind them Naiha let out an almost deranged laugh. "A great man you are! Letting your daughter see that! Do you feel strong now, meri jaan?" "Better her see this than her drunken whore of a mother falling all over the place!" Spit flew from Zakaria's mouth and Naiha came around the table to where he was standing, "Me?! Me a whore?! You think I don't notice all the women who stare at you at all your oh so important banquets?! Why do you think I drink, you idiot? Who could stomach that sober?!" Her finger jabbed him in the chest and Zakaria stared at her for a moment, shocked at her words. And then he hit her across the face, hard.

Naiha crumpled and lay on the floor stunned, a trickle of blood from her lip darkening the already dark fur of the rug in the room.

"I am giving you talaq." He spoke quietly from above her, she didn't look up at him. Instead, she listened as his footsteps moved towards the door, and then left the room. It was only then that she looked up. There was shattered glass on each end of the room, all three chairs were roughly pushed out around the table. Naiha brought her hand up to her lip to touch the cut, wincing at the contact. Very slowly, she got up, steadied herself, and walked out of the dining room.

She considered bringing Saba to her bedroom, but she couldn't let the girl see her in such a state. Instead, she went to the bathroom in her bedroom, splashed cold water on her face three times, and then sat on the toilet and cried.

Zakaria did not see Naiha until the following afternoon. Saba was still at school and Zakaria was tucking into his lunch when Naiha strode into the dining room with a short, grey bearded man who had a skull cap on his head behind her. "Who is this?" Zakaria didn't try to hide the annoyance in his voice. "He's a molvi from the mosque." "Well, did you bring him here to conduct a prayer?" He noticed that Naiha's bottom lip was visibly swollen and bruised, despite the attempt she had made to cover it up with makeup. A pang of guilt bit him in the stomach but it was quickly replaced with an air of defiance. "I'm asking you why he's here."

"For what you said."

"What did I say?"

"You said you wanted a talaq. You said it once. Go ahead and say it again, with him as my witness."

Zakaria was dumbfounded. He locked eyes with the old cleric, found a look of confusion and mild annoyance, and then chuckled. "You and your dramatics. You brought a molvi saab here for that?" "I'm not playing a joke, Zakaria. Say it again. What you said so boldly last night. Say it again so you can't hold it against me when you regret it. Let him be a witness. Go on."

"Is she serious?" Zakaria asked the old man. "Say it," she repeated, cutting off the cleric before he could say a word. At this, Zakaria's temper flared. "Fine! I give you a talaq. A talaq! Go to hell! And may you never again make such a miserable wife to anyone! Happy?!"

The molvi saab let out a hiss of disapproval, "Bite your tongue, son! Do you know what you're saying?!" "I'm saying what she wants! Let her hear what she wants!" Naiha was silent, watching the argument between Zakaria and the cleric take place. Neither one noticed when she smiled to herself, and it took a moment longer for them to notice that she had left the room. "There is still time to make this right!" The molvi saab said indignantly, but Zakaria waved away the words. "I am sorry my wife had to drag you into this charade of hers', molvi saab. I'm afraid she enjoys the drama. She will be back down here by tonight with a glass of wine in her hand. In fact, going to get you might have been the first time since we married that she's set foot in a mosque!" Zakaria burst out laughing, ignoring the worried look on the old man's face. Rasul Khan was summoned to escort the man back to the mosque, despite his protests.

When Naiha didn't come down for dinner that evening, Zakaria sent the servants to retrieve her from her bedroom. It was the maid who came running down the steps, pale in the face, clutching a note in her hands. It simply read;

"You have granted me my freedom. I will take full advantage of it. I know you love our daughter, and that you can provide a better life for her than I ever could. And so, I leave her in your care. I will pray every day that she finds a husband better than you.

-   *Naiha."*

Zakaria had clutched a chair to steady himself after reading the note and then immediately yelled at Rasul Khan to get to the airport and bring Naiha back. Half an hour later an agitated Rasul Khan had phoned to tell his master that his wife was nowhere to be found. Zakaria had cursed and called a contact of his who worked as an official at the airport, he had demanded the man check the logs to see where Naiha was. It hadn't taken very long. She had boarded a flight to Dubai, from there she was to be taken to America. It was too late, the man had explained, she would be sitting comfortably on her flight to New York City by now, and there was nothing that could be done to call the flight back. Zakaria had sworn at the man and then vowed to have the airport shut down. After hanging up he had paced back and forth furiously for a few moments before remembering the cleric. He drove himself to the mosque and barged inside, his eyes darted around before finally resting on the old man Naiha had brought to the house. "YOU!" he jabbed a finger into the old man's soft chest, "That woman, my wife. She paid you, didn't she? She paid you to come to our home yesterday?" The molvi saab rubbed the spot Zakaria had poked and regarded him coldly. "She is no longer your wife, sir. I tried to talk sense into you yesterday, but you did not listen to me. The young lady did not have to pay me, but I had to make sure that she was remembering what you'd said correctly. And then I heard you say it with my own ears, twice."

"And?! Doesn't there have to be a written contract or something?"

"Written or spoken, what does that matter? The Almighty was witness to your words no matter what form they were in. I even tried to warn you, and you would not listen. You knew what you were saying, and you said it anyway. Now you must wait. If she remarries and her next husband passes away or gives her talaq as well, then you may try to marry her again."

Zakaria fought the urge to spit in the mosque. "She's left me! She is on her way to America!"

"That is your own doing, sir."

Zakaria considered slapping the self-righteous bearded face, this short old man who was so clearly relishing in his torment. Instead, he swore, turned around, and went back home.

It took a year for Zakaria's fury and his confusion to ease. He had no connections in America, he could not get to Naiha no matter how much he wanted to. She would call occasionally, only to speak to Saba. If Zakaria snatched up the phone and began to speak into it, she would immediately hang up. It was new for his ego to be bruised like this. He had concocted a story about how she had been ill, enough people had seen her drinking habits, it wasn't difficult to create a story of her not being right in her mind around that. To say that she'd been sent to America for treatment, that Zakaria visited her twice a year when, in reality, his trips out of the country twice a year were to England or Saudi Arabia. But still, he knew that people had an idea of the truth. He could feel it in their stares, their whispers. He was no longer the son of Mehmood Bhatt, the powerful zamindar, he was now Zakaria Bhatt, the failed heir to his father's riches who couldn't even hang onto his own wife.

It was an insult to his pride, to his very manhood.

But his daughter had remained with him through it all. Saba, the one person he truly loved. She had known what differences existed between her parents, she known what her father had been as a husband, and yet she had loved him all the same. She would not betray him, he had thought.

And then she had come home one day with that boy, Khushal. A lower middle-class boy with a quiet demeanor. Nothing spectacular about him. He hadn't been incredibly good looking, he hadn't been highly educated either. But Saba had looked happy next to him, and the boy had the gall to come to Zakaria himself. He had admired this in the boy, and he might have agreed to the proposal if only for the sake of his daughter's happiness if it hadn't been for the fact that the boy's father had rejected Saba.

What special quality did the man deem himself or his son to have that justified a rejection of his daughter?

But once again, he had underestimated another's willingness to leave. He had gone up himself the next morning to speak to Saba and had found a neatly written note, similar to the one Naiha had left, telling him that she and the boy had left together to marry. Zakaria had waited until after he had burned the note, contacted the boy's family, called the police, and filed a kidnapping charge before he fell apart. Two days.

Two days before he had given into his rage and his sadness. He had spent most of the following few weeks in a drunken stupor. All business was put on hold. The reason given for this slight had been more easily believed by people. His daughter had been taken. His pride, his joy. The man had never done a thing except dote on her his whole life. Surely, she wouldn't have left home of her own accord. And yet somehow, even whispers of gossip can sometimes unknowingly contain seeds of truth. Perhaps one of the maids had passed it onto another family she worked for or perhaps told one of her companions who spread it around to the rest of the workers in the city, and they passed it onto their bosses. Either way, it did not escape Zakaria's notice that after some time had passed, people began to say that Saba *had*, in fact, run away with a stranger. She had fallen in love with a Hindu boy, some whispered, a union that couldn't be approved of at home by her Muslim father and so she had taken matters into her own hands. Others said that she had been bewitched by a Shia boy, some dark and blasphemous influence had been placed on her to draw her away from the loving home of her father. And others said that the boy had not been Shia, nor had he been a Hindu. He had simply been a low-class boy. Pitiful, unremarkable, and unworthy of marrying into a prominent family. This became the favorite theory, for how could anyone not be drawn in by the scandal of a girl leaving behind her father and the lavish life he had afforded her for a boy so clearly beneath her?

"Shameless, the girls of today are," said one old neighbor to her husband, "Absolutely shameless. And a fool that Zakaria Bhatt is. A good slap or two when she was growing up would've prevented this from happening, I'm sure. But of course, it's not entirely his fault. Or even the daughter's. Remember his wife? A woman like that becoming a mother? Something like this was bound to happen."

It was all this that finally pushed Zakaria to his breaking point. Saba would have to be punished. The wound of Naiha's insult had only just begun to fade, but the one inflicted by his daughter was not one he was sure would ever go away. "I'll kill her with my own fucking hands," he had growled to himself one night drunkenly, and then immediately regretted the notion after realizing what he was saying. It wasn't her. It wasn't her. It was the boy. The boy would have to be taught a lesson. But he couldn't kill the boy either, Saba wouldn't forgive him if she found out. But what if she didn't find out? What if he could find them, get the boy away from her, and force her to come home? And marry her off to a proper suitor? One of his choice? With her approval of course. Once she got over the pain of her first heartbreak, she would be agreeable again. The passions of youth were short lived anyway, Zakaria reminded himself, they did not last very long and the pain of them burned out just as quickly. He had convinced himself of this, so he had to find them. He had to punish Khushal, that was who had taken his daughter away from him. He would have to be found and then beaten or bribed until he himself relinquished her. Either that, or he would be killed. It made no difference to Zakaria, as long as Saba never found out. And so, he hired men who were under his employ specifically for tasks like this. If someone needed to be dealt with in a more personal, less formal manner, these were the men he called. He had sent them to every place that he could think of for where Saba might go. Old haunts of the family's, vacation homes, places where his own extended family lived, although he doubted that anyone of his own blood would have kept it from him if she had turned up. But what did he know anymore? Betrayal came easiest to family, it seemed.

But all would be right now.

Finally, Iftikhar and his men had found them. They had confirmed that it was Khushal, and they would bring him the boy soon.

Saba would return.

And finally, all would be right for Zakaria once more.

It was the first snowfall of the season. Big flakes drifted down lazily from the light grey clouds above and stuck to the trees, the grass, the roads, the buildings, everything. It was to pick up later in the week, it would get colder too and then it would begin to pile up. Everyone would get lazier, find any excuse to stay indoors as much as they could.

Khushal walked with his axe slung over his shoulder, the cold grass and leaves crunched ever so slightly underfoot. He had driven to the hills that he and Saba sometimes frequented and was now making his way into the woods. Classes had been cancelled, but Saba still had a meeting she needed to attend. She was to return late in the afternoon. He had wanted to sleep in that morning but had been woken by a dream. A stranger's face loomed in and out of the shadows, he had a look of deep concern on his face and he was saying something but Khushal couldn't hear him. The man in the dream had shoved a sheet of paper into Khushal's face, and that's when he had woken up. A tight feeling had settled under his right ear. That feeling he had felt, of something horrible about to happen, it was stronger today. He was sure that the dream had something to do with it. But he hadn't recognized the man. He hadn't been someone that Khushal or Saba knew personally, nor was he anyone that Khushal had seen in town.

He was worried, but over and over he reminded himself of the conversation he'd had with Saba. They would deal with it together, whatever it was. Once she came home, they'd speak about it. And both would be reassured once more.

Khushal pushed his thoughts to the back of his mind once he was deep enough in the woods. Someone would surely need extra firewood, and it wouldn't hurt to have some leftover for their own home either. It was better to be overprepared for the winters, they'd come to learn in the years since moving to the valley, than it was to be underprepared. Khushal planted his feet, gripped the axe tightly with both hands, and began to swing.

For fifteen minutes, there was no other sound except the thud of the axe as it sunk into the tree over and over, and Khushal's ragged breathing as he worked. He paused to wipe the sweat from his brow, which was beginning to steam in the cold air, and looked around. There had been the sound of something or someone walking nearby. Too loud for it to be the wind passing through the trees. Khushal looked to his left, searching for any sign of a presence in the forestry. He was about to turn and look in the other direction when the sound of heavy footfalls sounded behind him. Before Khushal could turn around and look, someone grabbed him from behind, trapping his arms at his sides.

"GET THE AXE!" The voice behind him yelled. Khushal yelled with rage and pushed himself backwards, throwing his head and his feet back. The back of his skull collided with a fleshy part of a face and the man holding him grunted, loosening his grip. But someone else had grabbed Khushal by the wrist and was trying hard to wrench the axe from his grip. Khushal spun around, moving both men with him and threw a kick in the direction of whoever was going for his axe. The man crumpled as Khushal's foot made contact. Before he could turn his attention back to the man who was holding him, someone's fist collided with the side of Khushal's head and his knees buckled. "TIE HIM UP! QUICK!"

Khushal felt someone grabbing at his hands now, attempting to tie them together and remove the axe from his hand. The man behind him had loosened his grip even more and Khushal seized his chance. He kicked back into the man's groin, tightened the grip on his axe, and swung upwards. Everything had happened so fast that he could barely see what was happening, but he felt the axe hit something, graze it, and there was a yell of pain. Khushal shook his head and rubbed it where the man had hit him, the man who was now laying on the ground and bleeding from where the axe had struck him on the shoulder.

Before Khushal could step forward and grab the man, someone else hit the back of his head with something hard and metallic. He spun on the spot, dazed, and suddenly felt a sharp pain in his abdomen. A short man with a blue shroud wrapped around his shoulders stood there, and in his hands he was clutching the hilt of the of the dagger he had stabbed Khushal with. Khushal stood there a moment, stunned. The taste of blood filling the back of his throat. And then his hands moved, he grabbed at the man's face, trying to dig his fingers into the man's eyes. The man let out a yell and stepped back, pulling the knife out of Khushal as he did. Khushal cried out in pain and swayed on the spot, his hands dropping to his stomach, moving in circles, trying instinctively to stop the blood. The bigger man who had first grabbed him from behind stood up, grabbed Khushal by his shoulders now and threw him down to the ground hard.

The cold earth sent a jolt of pain through Khushal's body and he groaned, arching his back while still clutching at the spot where he'd been stabbed. The men were moving above him now, muttering curses and whispering in worried tones. Khushal could make out none of it. His head throbbed dully as his hands and feet were tied. The big man lifted him up off the ground and Khushal groaned with pain as the man slung him over his shoulder, and his eyes began to close as he was thrown into the backseat of a truck.

The last thing he saw was the snow stuck to the window outside. The snowflakes twinkled like hundreds of little stars that were only a few inches away. And then he drew a sharp breath, and his eyes closed.

Laila barely made it to the bathroom in time. She almost collided headfirst with the toilet but steadied herself with her hands, clutching the edges of the bowl as she vomited. She remained in the position for moment, making sure the nausea had passed, before flushing and getting up to wash her hands and rinse her mouth out. Looking at herself in the mirror, Laila saw that there were yellow spots around her eyes and the eyes themselves were slightly bloodshot. She had been praying the afternoon prayers on her mat when she'd suddenly been overwhelmed with the nausea, it was all she could do to clamp her mouth shut, break her prayer, and dash to the bathroom. "Why did that happen?" Laila asked herself. For a wild, fleeting moment, she thought she was pregnant again. But then she remembered that that wasn't possible. She and Aziz had not been intimate for nearly a year now. Could it have been something she ate?

Laila turned over the questions in her mind. She felt uneasy, but she didn't know why. And for the first time in years, she wished that Aziz were home. She didn't know why. He wouldn't be any help if he were, he'd bark at her for being ridiculous and shove a pill into her hands for her to take to settle her stomach. But he was still her husband, even if just in name. At least there'd be someone else at home. She knew that if she insisted enough, he always came around to take how she felt seriously, however begrudgingly.

The trouble was, she did not know what exactly she was feeling. Her heart was beating faster than usual, and blood was pounding steadily in her ears. She splashed cold water onto her face and walked out of the bathroom and back to her prayer mat, grabbing her rosary off the coffee-table as she went. Laila sat down and began to pray again, with a focused intensity. All the words she whispered were directed at what she felt, whatever might be the cause of it. Despite the strange nature of it, Laila was sure that even this was not too strange to be tamed or helped by the words of her Creator.

The thought eased her heartbeat after a while, and she kept praying. The fingering of the rosary beads becoming meditative, the muttering of the old Arabic words putting her in a stupor.

Laila was so engrossed in what she was doing that Aziz had to shake her shoulders to snap her out of it when he came home four hours later.

The windows had frosted over, and the light of the fireplace refracted off it, giving it the look of a foggy drinking glass. Saba's shadow prevented the light from covering the whole window. Nearly a half hour had passed since Inspector Majid, two of his men, Hamza Mian, Aniqa-ji, and a couple more people from town who'd helped search had left her home. Still, Saba maintained her vigil by the window. Part of her still hoping, foolishly, she thought, to see him walking up the path to the front door. Axe slung over his shoulder, nose red with cold, laughing apologetically for his lateness. She would refuse to speak to him, and then she would yell at him for being so irresponsible, for driving her crazy with worry. And then she would forgive him. And they'd move on.

She blinked.

There was still nothing outside. Nobody walking up the path. No movement at all except for the snow falling and being blown around by the wind. She sighed and walked over to the couch, fell into it, and leaned back to close her eyes. The police and the men from town had found the jeep at the base of the hills she and Khushal often visited. "It did not look abandoned," Inspector Majid had said, "We are still searching. He might have fallen or gotten lost in the woods. The snow makes everything tricky. Don't lose hope yet. We will find him." He had placed a hand gently on top of Saba's and patted it clumsily to reassure her. "All of us will go back out first thing in the morning, beti. Right after prayers!" Hamza Mian had chimed in. "Khushal Babu is smart, Saba Jaan, he will be okay," Daoud the butcher had added.

The men had begun to leave when Aniqa-ji had taken Saba's hands into her own and kissed the backs of them. Saba had looked into the older woman's watery eyes and almost broken down. "It will be alright. He will be found. He is alright, I am sure of it. I can feel it in these old bones of mine. Khushal Babu is fine." She had then tried to convince Saba once more to eat something, and Saba had pushed around some of the now cold chicken stew and rice on her plate, balling up two mouthfuls and forcing herself to chew and swallow them so that the older woman would stop watching her.

The words of reassurance had not had the intended effect. The thought of Khushal out in the cold somewhere did not comfort her. Nor did she think that's what had happened. The snow had made it impossible to make out any footprints, the inspector had said, but they planned on going out the next morning with dogs to see if they could find him. She knew there were many underground caves deep in the woods, parts where the forestry was so thick that most people did not go past them for fear of getting lost or falling into one of the caves. Maybe that was where he had gone. He had been so worried lately, perhaps he'd kept walking. Giving himself time to think and, lost in thought, he had maybe fallen and gotten hurt. Or simply become lost....

Saba watched as Khushal stumbled in her direction, she stood up. Even in the dim light she could see the salt filled tears glittering faintly in his eyes. It pulled her own sadness to the surface, and she did not need words for it anymore. She went to him and put her arms against his chest to hold him up and he wrapped his arms around her, kissing her mouth and her eyes and her nose. She stepped to the side and they both sank into the couch, his head resting on her breast, his body shaking as he cried. His hair smelt of cold dirt and underneath that was the scent of the soap he had used that morning. Her own tears wove their way through the strands of dark hair, leaving silver streaks on his head. For years she had wondered why they had such an instinct for each other. Her mother had told her once in a drunken stupor that love was an illness, and it came with its own unnatural symptoms. Warping the senses and pulling them to new heights that were out of one's control. But she knew this was something more. And as Khushal lay there, holding her close to himself, he shared the thoughts that were going through her mind. He had been here before. If all had been written, how could he not have been? In the Book of the World, they had been drawn next to each other. The Great Artist's hand had trembled, and He had unintentionally drawn a line connecting the two of them. All breaths had been shared. All moments had been written in time with one another. How could they fight what had been created before Creation itself?

A log cracked in the fire and her eyes flew open, Saba looked around the room. There was no one there. She had dozed off, Khushal had not walked in. Quickly, she stood up and went over to the door, pulling it open and looking outside. Still, there was no one. He was not walking up the path, he was not stumbling in her direction.

Closing the door behind her, Saba went back to the couch, sat down, and finally began to cry.

III.

The quiet that had settled in the basement of the manor in recent weeks bothered Zakaria. Not that the noise would ever make its way up to the rest of the house. But for the first few weeks, while descending the stairs to the basement, he could always hear a grunt or a shout, maybe a curse or two. Sometimes even uninhibited cries of pain. But now there was nothing. There were no sounds at all. As he made his way to the door at the end of the narrow hallway, Zakaria reached into his pocket and pulled out a key. The room had not been used in years, and so the lock had stuck for the first few days, but now it clicked and opened up with ease. Pushing the door open, Zakaria stepped into the small room. Iftikhar was seated at the table, smoking a cigarette and peering down at a book with a pair of reading glasses on. Imran was crouched in the corner, holding a cup of water up to Khushal's lips. The boy's eyes had looked up in Zakaria's direction the moment he had stepped inside.

Zakaria had to admit to himself that it pained him to look at Khushal. His hair had grown long, it was dirty and matted down. His lips were cracked and dry, and he had lost an immense amount of weight. His face seemed hollow around the eyes, and nearly half his body was wrapped in bandages. They'd broken his legs, and he could no longer stand without help. And the right side of his face seemed permanently swollen. His clothes were worn and didn't fit him well anymore. They had changed him into a new set of clothes when he'd first arrived and burned the torn, bloody ones he'd been wearing. "Why didn't you just kill him?!" Zakaria had shouted at Iftikhar after seeing the knife wound in the boy's belly. "You wanted us to bring him to you, that is what we did." "Not half dead! If you were going to stab him you should've done so and left him there, that would have been the end of it! I'll have to pay off a doctor now, do you realize that?!"

"We had no choice," Iftikhar had regarded Zakaria coldly, "He had an axe with him. Haidar is going to need stitches, we're lucky he was only hit on the shoulder. Imran acted quickly when he stabbed him. You did not tell us that the boy carried an axe with him." "I'm supposed to know he's a fucking woodcutter?!"

In the end, Zakaria had a doctor from a small local clinic come to patch up Khushal's wounds as best he could. The man had been paid a generous amount of money for his silence and threatened as well. They had then restrained Khushal's hands and feet and put him in this room.

Khushal could only remember all of this in flashes. He had spent two days slipping in and out of consciousness and had believed that he was going to die for sure. But on the third day they had roused him, and he had felt with a grimace the stitching in his stomach. They planned on keeping him alive, for what, he hadn't known. Not until Zakaria had come into the room that day. Then it had become clear to Khushal. This was some form of revenge for marrying Saba, for running away. He had thought for a moment, or perhaps hoped, that they might simply beat him black and blue and then let him go. But that line of thinking quickly vanished when Zakaria had crouched down in front of him, looked him in the eye, and simply said, "Divorce my daughter."

The beatings had begun with his first refusal. Every day, one or two of the men would beat him. With their fists, their boots, sticks of bamboo, their belts, whatever they could do, they did. They broke his bones, they chipped two of his teeth, they slammed his head into the wall until he could feel something leaking inside. His stitches had come open one day when someone delivered a well-placed kick to his stomach. Khushal had sobbed with pain and thrown up blood. They had restitched him themselves as best they could and given him antibiotics for a week, holding off on beating him until he had recovered. They didn't want to kill him. They simply wanted him to divorce Saba. That is what he was told every day. The man Imran, the one who'd stabbed him, tried to convince him as gently as he could every day. "Just tell saab that you give his daughter talaq. This ends once you do. We let you go, you go home and start a new life. You don't like being in this much pain do you, bhai?"

Khushal had said nothing.

This was his usual response when Zakaria came into the room as well, asking if he would divorce Saba now. Khushal would glare at the man and say nothing, and eventually Zakaria would curse him and leave.

This day was different. Zakaria sat down in one of the chairs at the table and quietly told Imran to move. Khushal stared at Zakaria through the curtain of dirty hair that hung over his eyes. "Khushal. It pains me to see you like this. I do not enjoy making you suffer, I do not think you are a bad man. But Saba is my daughter. I love her, I would do anything for her. I want the best for my daughter. And I don't think that's what you are. She left the life she knew, a good life, to be with you. There is still time to undo that, for her to come back and live a life she's worthy of. Don't you want to give her that? This all ends if you just give her a talaq. She doesn't have to be here to hear it herself, tell us. We will be the witnesses. I will call her home. I will marry her to someone else. And you can go home, you can go home to your parents. You can start fresh yourself."

As Zakaria spoke, Khushal felt a weight pressing down on his chest every time he heard Saba's name. He let the man finish speaking but did not take his eyes off of him. Listening to every word. He remained silent for a moment after he had finished, and the words hung in the air. Imran and Iftikhar were both looking at him as well, waiting for an answer.

"You say you love her...," Khushal's voice was little more than a hoarse whisper, "If you loved her, you would know what she wants. I am in love with her. I always have been. I cannot give her a talaq. And even if I did, she would not come back to you. If you loved her, you would know that."

The response was the most Khushal had spoken in almost two months. Zakaria did not know if it was rage or confusion that he felt coursing through him. The boy was stubborn, he had expected him to be. But his words didn't just indicate a stubbornness. It was almost as if he didn't care what was happening to him. In truth, Zakaria could simply call Saba home once she gave up hope of finding Khushal. He had spoken to her for the first time in years about a week after the boy had been brought to the manor. She had cried that Khushal had gone missing and begged him to use his connections to help find him. Zakaria had felt joy at hearing her voice again, and he had listened to her quietly. Promising to do what he could. It had hurt to hear the pain in her voice, but he had convinced himself that it would pass. He did not know anymore, truly, why he carried on demanding the talaq from the boy. But he wanted to hear it. He

wanted to have the words come from Khushal's mouth. But now he was unsure
that they would come.

Khushal waited for Zakaria to say something, but he didn't. Instead, his
father-in-law shook his head, and walked out of the room. Iftikhar set down the
book he was reading.

"Love! All you young people do is speak of love. Do you even know what it
means?"

Khushal stared at Iftikhar for a second before laughing dryly. "Look at me,
Iftikhar Bhai. Do I look like someone who doesn't understand the weight of what
he's saying?" Iftikhar blinked and stared at him, Imran too was staring at him
with a peculiar expression on his face. "You don't understand. Neither of you
understand." Khushal licked his cracked lips. "You carry on doing what you're
doing to me because you don't understand. Maybe you could have once, maybe
you will later in your own lives. But it's plain to see that right now you don't. You
are not keeping me from her, you know. Maybe you *are* strong enough and cruel
enough beat me to the point of saying what you want me to say. But even then, I
will not be away from her. I am still there. That is where I am when you hit me.
That is where I go. Why would I care for what you do?"

Imran and Iftikhar both looked at each other and then once more at
Khushal, Iftikhar considered striking the boy to stop the nonsense. But something
was stopping him. Was it guilt? A sudden concern for the young man who
resembled a hunk of battered meat more than a man at the moment? He did not
know. And neither did Imran, who said nothing. Instead, he crouched down next

to Khushal again and held the cup up to his lips once more. "Drink." Khushal held Imran's gaze as he took a sip from the cup. Imran had to look away.

Six months passed. The window in the basement room that looked out into the back garden now hovered above the new Spring grass and unbloomed flowers. Every once in a while, Khushal could pull himself up to his feet with great effort using the wall for support and move as far as his restraints would allow him to look through the glass, catching a sliver of the horizon above which would sometimes contain a few stars, or sections of clouds. He could see the garden too, see servants coming and going through it, see guests that would sometimes stroll in it with Zakaria by their sides. It wasn't much, the window only about the size of a mail slot, but it somehow comforted Khushal to see what things looked like outside.

He was getting weaker. The skin around his eyes had tightened, his face was gaunt and had a long, unkempt beard hanging from it. His shirt slipped off his shoulders often. And the wound in his stomach had become infected. Khushal could feel it, though he didn't say anything to his captors. His stool would now either be discolored or contain large amounts of blood. Eating was painful, and so he did very little of it. Just enough to satisfy Imran when he would bring him his plate of food in the evenings. The beatings, as well as Zakaria's attempts to get Khushal to give Saba a talaq, had become incredibly infrequent. In fact, the only times Iftikhar and his men laid a hand on Khushal now was on days when they knew that Zakaria would be coming.

The sudden easing of his suffering surprised Khushal, he could not understand the reason for it. The men still cursed at him and yelled at him and slapped him occasionally, but it did not contain the same venom behind it.

"Just call your daughter home already," an irritated Iftikhar had said to Zakaria one day. "Is your job becoming too difficult for you, Iftikhar Mian? What am I paying you for?" In truth, Zakaria was now attempting to do exactly what was being suggested. And he was now worried about what he'd do with Khushal. He had not foreseen this happening the way it was. "Haidar is the only one who isn't tired of this now. And even that's just because he's still angry about the wound the boy gave him. It has been months. It's obvious that Khushal isn't going to give you what you want. Call your daughter and let him go or dispose of him. It is up to you."

"Khushal? You address him by his name so lovingly now, Iftikhar?" Zakaria stared at the man, who glared back at him with expressionless eyes. "This is your mess, you fool. If you want him dead so bad, you kill him yourself. You're not paying us enough for this. You didn't tell us your daughter ran off with him. You said that he took her against her will. Why is she still looking for him then?" "You will focus on what you're being paid for and nothing more. If you can't do the job, leave. There is a brainless jackass in every alley who would kill in exchange for half of what I'm paying you!"

Iftikhar had considered for a moment slapping the smug man across the face, but instead he glared at him for a few seconds before finally turning heel and walking out of the room.

Haidar was the one who left.

He had wrapped his belt around his fist and was beating Khushal in front of Zakaria one afternoon, demanding that he give the answer Zakaria asked for. And quite suddenly, he stopped, panting hard. Khushal had locked eyes with him, he had not made a sound throughout the beating, his body limp and resigned to move in whatever direction the force of the blows moved it. But his eyes made Haidar stop and step back. "Why'd you stop?!" Zakaria demanded to know. "This...isn't working. There's no point to this." Haidar slowly unwrapped the belt from around his hand. "What do you mean there's no point? Keep going!"

"No. Whatever you want from him, you aren't going to get it."

Zakaria slammed his own fist into Haidar's mouth, knocking him to the ground. "Get out of my house!" he spat. Haidar's lip bled freely as he pulled himself to his feet, he wiped his mouth with his sleeve and turned to look at Khushal again. The young man said nothing to him, but Haidar still felt the weight of something coming from him. "This, uh, this won't end well, Khushal. None of this will end well." Khushal let out a sigh. "We shouldn't have brought you here."

When Khushal didn't say anything to this, Haidar left the room, leaving a dumbfounded and furious Zakaria behind him.

Later he told Iftikhar that he had seen a "presence" in Khushal's eyes that afternoon. The beatings stopped entirely. Zakaria was not aware of this, they would put on a show for him when he came to the room, but both Iftikhar and Imran were careful to not cause Khushal any more pain. "Where is this kindness coming from all of a sudden, bhai?" Khushal had asked Iftikhar one evening after one of these displays. Iftikhar had no answer, he couldn't look at him without feeling shame. Imran now tended to Khushal as best as he could, feeding him with his own hands, and tending to the wounds. "This doesn't seem to be getting any better," he had said one evening, noticing the stained bandages wrapped around Khushal's stomach. "It's fine. I'm just dirty." When he replaced the wrappings with clean ones, Imran noticed the blackness of the wound, and how swollen it was. "Well, you tore the stitches with your beautiful boot, don't you remember?" Khushal had said with a smile when Imran asked him about it. Imran's face had flushed red and so Khushal added, "All is forgiven, Imran Bhai. Don't worry."

One night, as they were feeding him, Khushal finally said it out loud.
"I am dying." They froze and Khushal chuckled. "Oh, don't pretend we didn't all know it would go this way." He smiled sadly. "I cannot die yet though, I must see Saba one more time. I see her already, everywhere. There is not much I have to do to see her and speak to her. But I want her to be near me before I die."

Iftikhar cleared his throat. "Um, he should be calling her home soon. If you want we could, erm, we could...arrange something." The ramblings about seeing Saba everywhere were not new, both he and Imran had grown accustomed to hearing them by now, yet they still couldn't figure out how to react. They had convinced themselves that the young man had simply lost his mind. Their beatings had done it, and the guilt that came with that knowledge prevented both men from resting easy now. "What could you arrange? Imran Bhai, will you bring her down here to have dinner with me? You could feed us with your own hands." Imran remained silent as Khushal laughed at his own joke. "What would you like us to do, Khushal?" Iftikhar asked.

"I do not know yet. I will tell you once I do. But I didn't want to hide it from you anymore, it was becoming too tedious. Besides, you two men are the closest things I have to friends now."

One night, Imran roused Khushal from a dream. He had been with Saba by their fireplace, rubbing her shoulders and kissing the back of her neck gently as she leaned back against him. "Khushal, Khushal please, I need to ask you something." Khushal groaned and pulled himself up into a sitting position, hand instinctively fluttering towards the wound. The smallest movements now sent a searing pain through his whole body. "What is it, Imran Bhai? You interrupted a good dream." "I am sorry." Imran looked away and then back at Khushal, "I am sorry for much more than just that." Khushal was going to laugh when he noticed the sweat on Imran's face, and the genuine panic in his eyes. "What is wrong?"

"I told you. I am sorry. I am so sorry, Khushal. I shouldn't have stabbed you."

"I would have preferred that myself. Although, I *did* try to gouge your eyes out, so I can't say I blame you."

"Please, be serious, Khushal." The smile fell from Khushal's face and he stared at the trembling man in front of him, reaching out, Khushal placed a hand on his shoulder. Cold sweat was staining the shirt. "We shouldn't have gotten involved. I am so sorry. I am incredibly sorry. We didn't know. Zakaria didn't tell us the truth, he told us you stole his daughter." At this, Khushal smiled. "A human being can never be something to steal, Imran Bhai." "I know. I know that, now. But even then, we had no idea what we would be destroying. Did you know that Haidar has stopped speaking since he left on that last day with you? His mother told Iftikhar and I that he barely eats anymore, and never speaks. He spends all of his time going to the mosque, praying. He doesn't work. She's worried. She thinks someone has cursed him, she thinks her son has lost his mind."

"I promise you, I did no such thing. I did not wish you or any of your partners any ill will. I have not done that once since I've arrived here. And I am very sorry to hear that is happening." Imran shook his head, "I know. I know it's not you, we've seen what you are. What you're like. Never for a moment could we think you did that. But it's what's happening because of what we did to you. To you and to the girl, to Saba. By bringing you here. Khushal, please. Please forgive us. I am so sorry. I am so so sorry I didn't know. We didn't know..." Imran's voice trailed off and he began to sob quietly, the shoulder shaking under

Khushal's hand as he watched this small man begging him for forgiveness. Khushal had not lied about not wishing the men ill, but he had hated them when they'd first brought him to this place. He'd hated them when he realized what the reason was. But he had exhausted that months ago. He did not feel much of anything for them anymore, not good nor bad. But now, watching Imran cry, he felt a twinge of pity. "I will say a prayer for you, Imran Bhai. You, and Iftikhar, and Haidar. All of you. I might even say one for my delightful father-in-law. A dying person's prayers have more weight for Khuda Saab, I think."

Imran hiccupped and sniffled, looking up at Khushal with bleary eyes, "I wish you weren't dying here."

"I will not die until I see Saba. I am saying that to you because it is the truth. If I see her again, I will die. And it will be painless. Until that happens, I'll hover in this painful in between. You say she's coming soon?" Imran nodded. "Yes. She is coming in two days." Khushal smiled. "Then I have two more days to live. Don't be sad, Imran Bhai. And do not be so hard on yourself. You are not the only one between the two of us who has sinned greatly." "What could you have possibly done?!" Imran asked indignantly.

"Was I not careless? I cared only for what I wanted, which was Saba. I thought that we could leave everything behind for each other."

"So did she! She left with you."

"Yes, so did she. But she is not the one in this room, is she? No. She is the one suffering not knowing what is happening. I can feel it, you know? In my head. In my whole body. Her pain feels like a weight on my whole body. How can I care for my own when I feel only hers'? We both were careless. And because of that carelessness, there will now be a mother without a son. A father without a son." Khushal smiled sadly, "There will be a woman who is widowed."

"You fell in love with each other, Khushal. Since when do things like carelessness or carefulness play a factor in something like that?"

"I was a fool about it. It is foolish to believe that the world we are in will not seek to uproot something like that. That it will allow it to thrive. Such a thing can never reach its full potential here, Imran Bhai. It blossoms fully somewhere else."

Imran didn't know how to respond to this. "You think I'm mad, I know you do. You think I have lost my mind. I promise you, I haven't. I am sane. I know what I am saying. I do not know what you make of it. Nor do I know what those who will hear about this after it all comes to an end will say about me, or Saba, or what we shared. I don't know how much of it will be truth and how much will be gossip. But if there is a world beyond this, a life after this one, whether it takes place here once again, or whether it takes place someplace so far off we can only imagine it, I will find Saba again. I will wait for her. She'll come to me herself. We have always found each other. We always will. That is not something you can destroy. Nobody can destroy that, Imran Bhai."

Imran listened to Khushal silently and nodded, "I understand," he said, not knowing what else to say. "You don't. But one day, you will." Khushal and Imran held each other's gaze a moment before Khushal yawned, "I am tired, Imran Bhai. If there's nothing else you would like to talk about, I'd like to go back to sleep." "Of course. We will speak more in the morning." Imran stood up and dusted himself off, Khushal watched the door gently swing shut behind him, and then he rolled over onto his side, staring up at the bottom of the window. The light pink tinge of early morning light was brushing against the window before Khushal drifted off.

The night before Saba's arrival, Khushal thought about Amma before going to sleep. He had avoided it since being brought to the manor. He didn't want to risk worrying her by letting her know what was happening. But he could now. He was sure of it.

The bedroom was exactly how he remembered it. The curtain was parted slightly to let a sliver of moonlight into the room. Laila and Aziz both still slept in the same positions as well. Nothing had changed. The corners of the room were drowned in shadows, but that was okay. Seeing what he needed to see was enough. Amma's face swam in front of Khushal, her eyes were closed, and a few stray strands of hair were falling over her face. He wanted to move them, but he couldn't. Instead he just watched her for a moment, and then leaned and brushed his lips against her forehead. She didn't move. Instead, she slowly faded away.

Khushal looked up towards what remained of the bed, Aziz was sleeping with his back to him. There wasn't much left to do, Khushal went around to his father's face. The brow was furrowed slightly even in sleep. Perhaps they would get another chance, the one they'd received this time had not done either of them much good. Aziz's face swam in front of Khushal, and he reached out, placing a hand gently on the side of it. This was the most he could do.

Aziz slowly faded away as well. For a moment the glow of moonlight remained, and then that faded out as well. There was only darkness now. Khushal felt himself being pulled back.

"Khushal. It's almost time." His eyes opened.

Iftikhar stood in front of him. Khushal looked up at the man and smiled, Imran undid the restraints and he almost fell over. Both men moved forward to catch him and hold him up. "Like I said, my only two friends," Khushal laughed weakly. "Do you want to eat anything?" "No. I couldn't stomach it anyway." "I will bring her to you," Iftikhar said. "Once she arrives, I will bring her here."

He left the room to go upstairs to the main part of the house where he would be able to see the driveway through the window, and Imran was left alone with Khushal. They did not speak. Khushal couldn't bring himself to. He was nauseous, and his eyes were playing tricks on him. So were his ears. He was seeing her every time he blinked and hearing her voice as well. But she wasn't here yet. He had to keep reminding himself. She was not here.

He was not aware of how much time passed by, but after a while, he could hear her clearly. Khushal stood up, Imran looked at him. "What's wrong?" "Saba's here," breathed Khushal. Imran stood there, confused, Khushal pushed past him and moved towards the window, clutching the sill and looking out into the garden.

She was there.

She had on a turquoise dress, and the scarf draped loosely over her head had silver flowers stitched into it. He could see clearly her eyes, her nose, her mouth. Her face may as well have been inches from his own. She had been drained, just as he had been. Her clothes barely hung onto her body, her walk resembled a drunken stupor. But it was Saba.

Khushal's breath caught in his chest. "Saba..." he whispered. And the window pulsed in front of him, he stepped back, letting out a ragged breath as a fresh wave of pain tore through his whole body. Imran lunged forward and caught him in time, before his head hit the floor. Khushal was shaking, and his body was drenched in sweat. "IFTIKHAR! IFTIKHAR! QUICK! COME QUICK!"

The yells were reduced to a dull throbbing in Khushal's ears, he couldn't hear them clearly. He couldn't see clearly either. The ceiling had begun to glow a blinding red color. And Saba's face hung there through it all, above his own. Her dark hair was tickling his eyes, his nose, his cheeks, his chin. He could feel it.

It was okay, he thought to himself. This would not hurt for much longer. Already, the pain in his body had eased, his muscles had relaxed. Someone was holding his head in their lap, but he didn't know who it was anymore.

He didn't know anything anymore.

There were words trying to crawl to his lips, someone had to hear them. It was important that someone hear them. But sound did not crawl with them. Imran was still yelling for Iftikhar.

He did not see that Khushal's lips were moving.

They moved in a soundless whisper. And then they stopped.

Zakaria watched from the window in the study as the car pulled into the driveway. Saba was inside of it. He smiled to himself and stepped away from the window, heading to the back-garden courtyard now to meet her. It did not matter anymore, what had happened. She was back. She was home. The boy could be thought about later. If Iftikhar and his man did not have the fortitude to kill him, Zakaria would do it himself. Or maybe he could have the boy institutionalized someplace. No one would know who he was, he would not be a problem again.

Whatever it was, it could come later.

Right now, he had to see Saba. That was all that mattered.

Saba felt a smile tugging at the corners of her mouth when she saw her father step out through the doors into the garden. He was exactly how he remembered him, only a little greyer now. She might have cried if the energy for it had been present, but it hadn't been there for weeks. Or perhaps she was simply too exhausted to feel anything at all anymore. Abba had assured her that he had hired a few top detectives himself to find Khushal, and that if they heard anything they would let him know. His willingness to help had surprised her. "I do not agree with your choices, meri jaan. But if it'll ease your pain, I am more than willing to help," he had said. Saba had not thought he would ever be so sincere with her again after she left. Perhaps she had underestimated him. And maybe once Khushal was found, Abba would feel differently about their marriage. This is what she hoped.

He had convinced her to come home, to rest. And it wasn't until she'd spoken to her mother that Saba agreed to come. "For all the things that man is, he does love you, Saba." Mama was been sincere in saying this, it was something she'd said to Saba countless times before.

She almost didn't notice that she had crossed the garden, it wasn't until Zakaria grabbed her and pulled her into a tight embrace that she snapped out of her thoughts. Saba's arms went up and returned the hug. "I've missed you so much," said Zakaria. Before Saba could respond, her head spun, and she pushed herself away from him. Zakaria stared at her, alarmed, while she stumbled backwards and leaned over, clutching her knees to support herself. She was breathing heavily, and her eyes were red, tears streaming from them. A strangled sound came from her throat and she retched, nothing coming up, but the world was spinning. She sank into a crouch and clutched her head with both hands, her breathing shallow all of a sudden. "Saba! Saba, what's wrong?" Zakaria placed a hand on her back and she moved away from him again, trying to stand back up, wiping at her mouth with her sleeve. She didn't know what was happening, she tried to say something, and as she looked up to speak to Abba she noticed a large man running in their direction, coming from around the side of the house. He was waving frantically.

Zakaria noticed him as well and a coldness set into his eyes, Saba noticed it. "Abba," she said, getting back up to her feet slowly. He looked at her, and she bristled. Taking a step backwards, her eyes darted around the garden. Everything was still spinning and she could hear something now, very faintly. It was so quiet she couldn't be sure she was hearing it, but she was sure that she was. It was her name. Someone was whispering her name.

"What's happened, Abba?" she asked, "What did you do?"

One afternoon a year later, Saba looked around the cottage. Aniqa-ji had just left, her chipped teacup was still resting on the coffee-table. She had planned on reorganizing the bookshelves today, since it was her day off, but when she'd woken up that morning she found that she did not have the energy for it. The school is what kept her busy most days now, but she did not know how much longer she would stay, if she wanted to at all. There had been a position offered to her from a university in the capital, the letter sat on the kitchen counter with the rest of the mail, she had not given them an answer yet.

The upcoming weekend, she would visit Laila and Aziz. It had become a monthly practice now. To go and spend a weekend with them. Sometimes they all had much to say, and sometimes they would all sit around and drink chai, lost in thought. Aziz's reception of Saba was much warmer now, more than she could ever have imagined. It almost worried her, this newfound gentleness. With it came what seemed like a rapid form of aging. He was losing his teeth at an alarming rate, and his beard was almost entirely grey.

Laila was different too. Similar to how Saba was. She didn't say much, she didn't need to. The weight of her pain was evident in everything. How she moved, how she spoke, how she sat, how she ate, how she slept. Saba knew that the pain they shared bonded them, but that did not make it any easier to speak about.

Still, it comforted her to see them. To see that there were still parts of his life that existed. It made her feel less alone.

Mama had convinced her finally to visit her in America the following month. Saba knew it broke her mother's heart the first few months, when she could do nothing to help except listen to Saba cry on the phone. Perhaps seeing her would make her feel better, but even that she wasn't entirely ready for. It had been over a decade, she wondered if she would even recognize Mama anymore. She'd seen pictures over the years, of course, but who knew if the real thing would be something she could spot instantly?

Saba stepped outside and looked around. The last of the Spring breezes were passing through these days. Soon, it would be Summer. The air would be thick with heat and the valley would be dense with flowers of all sorts. But for now, the breezes still passed through, the air was pleasant, and as for the flowers, they were still budding, their colors not yet fully formed. The slivers of undeveloped peeked out in the sunlight while they moved with the gentle winds. She went around to the back of the cottage, walking a few feet before coming to a stop at the headstone. When she had learned what had happened, Saba had thought she would have to beg Laila and Aziz to let her bury Khushal behind the home they shared together. It hadn't been necessary. They hadn't argued against it, they didn't seem to have the energy to. And they had not reserved any plots for their family in the local cemetery, so there was no reason why Saba couldn't bury him where she wished.

She had washed his body herself, there had not been much of an attempt to stop her. By law, their marriage ended when Khushal died, and so she could no longer look upon his naked body as that of her husband's. But the cleric had not had the heart to argue against it after taking one look at the brokenhearted girl's face. It reminded him quite suddenly of a heartbreak he himself had suffered under much different circumstances nearly half a century before. The wounds he had suffered had left him almost entirely unrecognizable. Even after removing the beard that had grown on his face, Saba could see only a glimmer of the Khushal she'd committed to memory. His bruises, his cuts, and bent bones had seemed to vibrate under her touch, but she had ignored this feeling. He was gone, and nothing of him remained in the body.

With one hand, Saba reached out to touch the cold stone, passing her fingers over it. Already, time had begun to weather the material. Cracks had begun to form, and the upper left corner had a small piece that had been chipped away.

He visited her dreams.

Whenever she slept, Khushal would be there waiting for her in the darkness. This might have made her happy if she didn't have so much trouble falling asleep now. She tried with sleeping pills, she tried by overworking herself, she tried everything she could, but sleep still came with great difficulty. And so too did her meetings with Khushal.

She could still recall that day in Abba's garden, the whisper she'd heard, it had been him. Somehow, she knew this to be true, even though she had no way of explaining how she knew it. Another breeze passed over her and Saba closed her eyes, listening so that she might hear it again.

The grass tickled her legs where she crouched.

And she waited.

She waited.

Made in the USA
Middletown, DE
16 October 2022

12876850R00045